FEB - - 2020

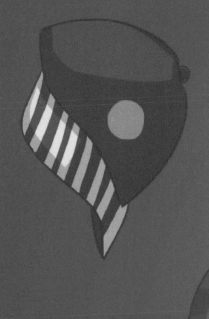

Jessie's Hat Collection

By Nick Barnes

Jessie has a huge hat collection.

When she gets a new hat, she always bends the brim.

Her favorite hats are baseball caps.

She loves sports and watches games
with her dad.

When she plays sports, she likes to wear her cap backwards.

Jessie doesn't like to take her hat off,
even in the bath.

She wears blue jeans and t-shirts, and, of course, hats.

Last Easter Jessie's mom made her take off her hat and wear a dress. Jessie cried and cried.

One of her favorite hats is camouflage. She likes to wear it when she plays army with her brother.

Sometimes Jessie wears her train engineer's cap. She thinks trains are cool.

Jessie's friends are mostly boys. Her best friend is Ben.

At school, she wears a hat whenever it's allowed.

The other girls don't wear hats, but
Jessie doesn't seem to notice.

Sometimes her classmates point and laugh at her behind her back. She doesn't know why.

Another kid at school made fun of her for looking like a boy.

Later that night, Jessie asked her parents why she was a girl and not a boy. She told them, "I really want to be a boy!"

Jessie's parents hugged her and said she can be a boy if she really wants to be.

Jessie was so excited that she decided to bring two hats to school the next day, one hat for the morning, and one hat to wear after lunch.

She told her friend Ben that she was now a boy. Ben said, "I kinda figured," and they both laughed.

One of her classmates pointed at her and called her a boy. Ben said, "Yeah, so what?"

The other students saw this and came over to talk to Jessie. The kids were curious and asked lots of questions.

Jessie didn't have all the answers, but knew one thing for sure, that he was meant to be a boy and not a girl.

CPSIA information can be obtained
at www.ICGtesting.com
Printed in the USA
LVHW071626300120
645334LV00001B/13